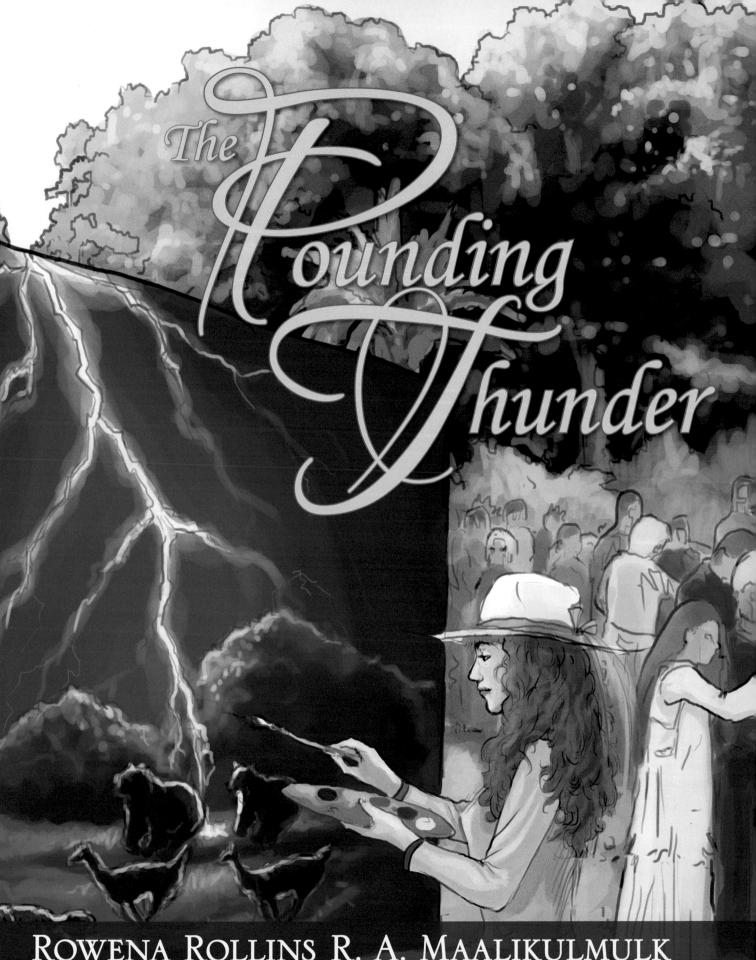

The Pounding Thunder

Rowena Rollins R. A. Maalikulmulk

Illustrated by: Ivan Earl Aguilar

Lightning strikes upon the Valleys as the insects and the animals run into their shelters. Within their habitats they turn close to each other trying to keep warm from the cold breeze. Stillness comes upon the Earth as it embraces the enormous clouds above changing its forms into purple, blue, and black. It was a picture of a painting done by an Artist that only a viewer can imagine.

As The Artist paints upon the canvass the picture becomes alive. And the life within it forms and circulates; blending into the tones and shades of its surrounding. As the audience become involved they witnessed The Artist's performance of The Arts of imagination; and they were astound by the Artist's painting, taking on its own meaning, and fascinating the eyes of its viewers!

Behold ...The Making the Art of each stroke, each brush, and each dip into the paint was done precisely in detail. As a gifted reader would have made in a complexity of a story.

What flair, what dexterity, what surmountable imagination that one couldn't tell that The Artist was blind and deaf. For she is not limited by her nature of her condition and she finds it a challenge to overcome her difficulties.

She sees and feels with her hands. And with the touch of an object she feels its vibration and its texture. And just by touching the paint itself she knows its colors and paint portraits exactly the way it is on canvas!

When I walk, she hears my foot steps and when I call her, she answers.

Today she placed her hands upon my face and drew my picture. I was surprise about how she painted my

Colored face complexion brown and what I was wearing, a blue t-shirt and white pants.

Then she made me smile just yesterday when she told me that she heard my conversation over the phone. I was surprised! "You did!" I said.

"No not really ... you know I'm blind and deaf, but I do have a good sense of humor!" She chuckled. "For I find that life is a Blessing and I'm Honor that Allah has given me a gift that I can appreciate and share with others!"

"*With Difficulties there is ease! And that's how Allah (SWT) makes it a way for everybody in each and every situation! And I don't feel that I have to give up anything more than anybody else! But at times, I do have a problem with getting around in a new area, but that can be expected."

She picked up her paint brush and drew a deer under a tree and her fawn hiding in the grass while it was raining and thundering. I asked her how she knows which colors to use and how she can blend these colors together to get the right position when putting it on canvas.

And she responded, placing her hands on the canvas, "I envision the picture in my mind. And I blend those colors by asking my friend to lighten or darken the colors for me; and number them with a printed code that I can feel the forms with my fingers. So ...I place them according to their shades from light to dark, making the color codes marks the light that I read with."

She picked up some color painted jars and placed them in my hands. "Can you feel the color codes on the side of these lids?" She said, as she pointed to them one by one. "This one is blue, this is white, and this one is black." "Yes, I do!" I said,

"And it feels like some sort of round dots pressed against my fingers, are these alphabets for you?"

I asked.

"Yes, indeed!" She said, "And with a lot of practice," she continued, "I became better and it sort of flowed easier for me as time went by. And boy ... I was moving with speed and no one could stop me! For Almighty God Allah Blessed me with talent and I knew that He was preparing me for my future. And I couldn't deny the Mercy and Blessing that Allah has given me!

So ... I pursued my course and Now I'm An Artist and the rest is History!"

She took the paint jars out of my hands and placed them on the edge of the painting along with the paint brushes and a glass of water. "And surprise ... this one is for you!" she exclaimed, opening up her left hands and pointing to the painting. "For it comes a time in everyone's life that God blesses the child that got its own!"

As she picked up the painting and placed it against her chests she reached out her hands and placed it in mine. "I like you to have this picture for I see that you would love it!" she said, while she finishes writing her signature at the bottom.

"Oh! Thank You!" I said, as she placed the painting in my hands, "I'll always remember You and Your Gifted Hands May Allah Bless You for Your Kindness!" I said, as I was delighted and my face blushed with a warm feeling of joy and aspiration.

"For What she couldn't see with her eyes she must have felt with her heart," I thought, "because I really did love and want this painting." My heart was pounding and my hands were trembling; as the tears ran down my cheek for I was overcome with joy by this gift. I stood there momentarily captivated by the thought of how blessed I was; that Allah had given me the opportunity see this day, and that I could hear the sounds of life and music around me!

I looked up at the sky and the clouds like I never saw them before and felt the brilliant rays of the sun. I could hear the sounds of the birds singing and the harmony of their voices and I was moved by it. For the first time in my life I felt alive; and that I had a purpose in life, and this day was my day, that I would thank God Allah for what He has given me!

I thanked The Artist and went away exploring the market place. Could I be like the Fawn in The Painting taking on the world around me? And it all became clear … that I was going to be someone special! Like the bird that leaves its nest in the morning empty and comes back full!

For Today, I would take the opportunity to see What Allah Created through The eyes of an Artist. I took my painting and walked over the bridge and I noticed how the boats and the buildings blended and combined with colors and shades.

And the trees, I was amazed by its varieties of colors being green, red, yellow, and purple. I knew that I would have to spend some time in the library to find out what kind of trees they were!

I walked for miles looking at people and their families; and noticed their different types of traditional clothing, and the food they were eating. The more I looked; the larger the picture was, and the more I wanted to learn. My mind was full and there was still more to come.

To my left, to my right, up and down; in and out of sight was life going on, in and out, and around me. The more I saw the more I didn't know? And what is this thing and what is that? It was looking like a mixture of fruits and vegetable gardens! And it made me think of how Allah's Earth was spacious and The Following Surah expressed in The Holy Qur'an ..., "Which of the favors of Thy Lord can You Deny?"

I sat by the rocks at 31st street beach in Lake Michigan looking towards Down Town Chicago. I began dreaming that I was in Paris traveling and viewing The Eiffel Tower. And Flying to Italy and was astounded by the appearance of The Leaning Tower of Pisa and The Next stop London Bridges … Big Ben and The Royal Palace waving at The Queen!

"And maybe I will go to Mecca if I'm not too young or travel to The Empire of Japan on a donkey! Endless Possibilities," I thought, as the clouds changed its colors. I felt the cool drops of rain upon my face and the chills came over me.

"It's Time to go Home!" I thought, as I began to dream of the sweet smelling mowed grass after it rain; that I would rest comfortably thinking of my adventure, and the places I'll go, and The people I'll meet.

I heard The cracks Of Thunder and The

Roaring Winds; as One, Two, Three, drops of rain fell on the ground, and there was more to come.

So …I put on My coat and ran skipping all the way home as it started to rain and thunder. I arrived at my house soaked and wet and hanged up my coat. And walked up the stairs to my room and placed the painting on my wall. Then I stood back and laid on my bed; and named it The Pounding Thunder, and went to sleep with a smile on my face.

And Guess What? It Rained and Thundered all last night and I didn't even … budge, because it only reminded me of My Painting …The Pounding Thunder!

Sign by The Artist,

Mahalia Jackson Belinda Ali

P.S.

For Allah gave me a Gift

That I could Appreciate!

Rowena Rollins Raheal A. Maalikulmulk

May Allah Bless those that are Gifted and share their talent with others and help them develop into productive citizens that take on the world! And evolve like being motivated to respond and astound the community by living in this World like that of an Artist. And living the Life of being a Muslim; enjoying Allah's Creation, and painting in details of what they see. Surprising the eyes of its viewers …

and captivating the moment …
and making your own picture …
and producing your own results,
With The Will of Allah!

As–Salaamu-Alikum!

Peace and Blessings,

~Rowena Rollins Raheal A. Maalikulmulk~

Print information available on the last page

Rev. date: 03/31/2015

Illustrated by: Ivan Earl Aguilar

To order additional copies of this book, contact:
Xlibris
1-888-795-4274
www.Xlibris.com
Orders@Xlibris.com

Printed in the United States
By Bookmasters